How to Make
Friends
with a
Giant

GENNIFER CHOLDENKO

Illustrated by

AMY WALROD

G. P. Putnam's Sons

G. P. PUTNAM'S SONS

A division of Penguin Young Readers Group. Published by The Penguin Group.

Penguin Group (USA) Inc., 375 Hudson Street, New York, NY 10014, U.S.A.

Penguin Group (Canada), 90 Eglinton Avenue East, Suite 700, Toronto, Ontario, Canada M4P 2Y3 (a division
of Pearson Penguin Canada Inc.). Penguin Books Ltd, 80 Strand, London WC2R oRL, England. Penguin Ireland,
25 St. Stephen's Green, Dublin 2, Ireland (a division of Penguin Books Ltd.). Penguin Group (Australia),
250 Camberwell Road, Camberwell, Victoria 3124, Australia (a division of Pearson Australia Group Pty Ltd).
Penguin Books India Pvt Ltd, 11 Community Centre, Panchsheel Park, New Delhi - 110 017, India.
Penguin Group (NZ), Cnr Airborne and Rosedale Roads, Albany, Auckland 1310, New Zealand (a division of
Pearson New Zealand Ltd). Penguin Books (South Africa) (Pty) Ltd, 24 Sturdee Avenue, Rosebank,
Johannesburg 2196, South Africa. Penguin Books Ltd, Registered Offices: 80 Strand, London WC2R oRL, England.

Published simultaneously in Canada. Manufactured in China by South China Printing Co. Ltd.
Design by Gunta Alexander. Text set in Equipoize Sans Bold.

Library of Congress Cataloging-in-Publication Data
Choldenko, Gennifer, 1957-   How to make friends with a giant / Gennifer Choldenko ; illustrated by Amy Walrod.
p. cm.   Summary: The other kids make fun of the new boy because he is so tall, but his short classmate Jake
helps him fit in. [1. Size—Fiction. 2. Schools—Fiction. 3. Friendship—Fiction.] I. Walrod, Amy, ill. II. Title.
PZ7.C446265 Ho 2006   [E]—dc21   2001048727   ISBN 0-399-23779-8   10 9 8 7 6 5 4 3 2 1   First Impression

To Ian and Kai —G. C.

For Ervin, a giant in spirit and creativity —A. W.

My mom is short.

My dad is short.

My dog is short.

I'm short too.

I don't like being short.

One day, workers come next door.

They make everything taller.

Then movers carry lots of big stuff inside.

The next day at the bus stop, I see a new kid.

Ann and Ed see him too.

"He's big," Ed says.

"He's a giant," Ann says. "A giant kid."

"A kid giant," Ed says.

"Either way, he doesn't belong," Ann says.

The new kid stands alone.

"Hey!" I say. "Did you just move next to me?"

The new kid closes one eye. He holds his thumb and finger close together. "Your dog chew teeny tiny dog bones?" he asks.

I hold my arms wide apart. "Your dog chew big, enormous dog bones?"

He nods his head. "My name is Jacomo."

"My name is Jake," I say. "I'm in first grade."

"Me too," Jacomo says.

"Want to sit by me?" I ask.

"Sure," says Jacomo.

"Look, Ed!" Ann says. "The shrimp and the giant are friends."

When the bus comes, Jacomo tries to get on.

He stoops down.

He squats low.

But Jacomo can't fit through the bus door.

Ann and Ed laugh.

"Can't you help?" I ask the bus driver.

The bus driver shakes his head. "What can I do?"

"The giant has to walk! The giant has
        to walk!" Ann says.

I get a seat. Then I get an idea. "Jacomo, you want
        to race?" I call out the window.

When the bus gets to school,
Jacomo is waiting.
"He beat us," Ann says.
"Yes, he did," I say.

Jacomo is big for Room 7.

He is big for the door and the chairs too.

Miss Sam is our teacher.

Jacomo is bigger than Miss Sam.

"Miss Sam, this is Jacomo," I say.

Jacomo lifts up Miss Sam to say hello. Miss Sam's
    shoes drop off.

"Put me down, Jacomo," Miss Sam says.

Jacomo puts her down.

"Jacomo, are you sure you're in first
    grade?" Miss Sam asks.

Jacomo shows Miss Sam his room slip.

It says Room 7.

Miss Sam writes a new rule on the board.

"No dangling the teacher in the air."

"Where should Jacomo sit?" I ask.

"Sit in front, Jacomo," Miss Sam says.

"He's blocking everyone," Ann says.

"Sit in back, Jacomo," Miss Sam says.

Jacomo sits in back.

I sit with Jacomo.

We work all morning.

Then it's carpet time.

Jacomo gets down on the carpet.

His head bumps the mobile. His elbow knocks
      the fish tank.

"There's no room," Min says.

"Where do we sit?" Jim asks.

"Jacomo is too big," Jeff says.

"Jacomo belongs in another school. A school
      for giants," Ann says.

Jacomo's lip trembles.

His shoulders shake.

"Look," I say. "We can make room."

Jim sits down.

Min sits down.

Ann crosses her arms. "None of the other
   classes have to do this."

"Just sit down, Ann," I say, "and be quiet."
Miss Sam reads the book.
Jacomo doesn't cry.

At recess we play soccer.

Ed and Min are captains.

Jacomo is Ed's first pick.

I am Min's last pick.

Jacomo kicks the ball.

He makes the goal, but the ball doesn't stop.

It sails over the trees.

The ball is gone.

The game is over.

"Did you have to kick so hard?" Ed asks Jacomo.

"Tomorrow you'll be last pick. Just like Jake."

"Jacomo," I say. "You're a great player.

You just have to kick softer."

"I can't," he says. "I forget."

"Give me a piggyback," I say.

"See that pinecone?" I whisper in his ear.

"Kick it soft, soft, soft."

Jacomo kicks one pinecone, two, three.

Ed, Ann and Min watch.

Four, five, six, seven.

Each pinecone makes the goal.

"Tomorrow you'll be first pick, Jacomo," Ed says.

"You and Jake."

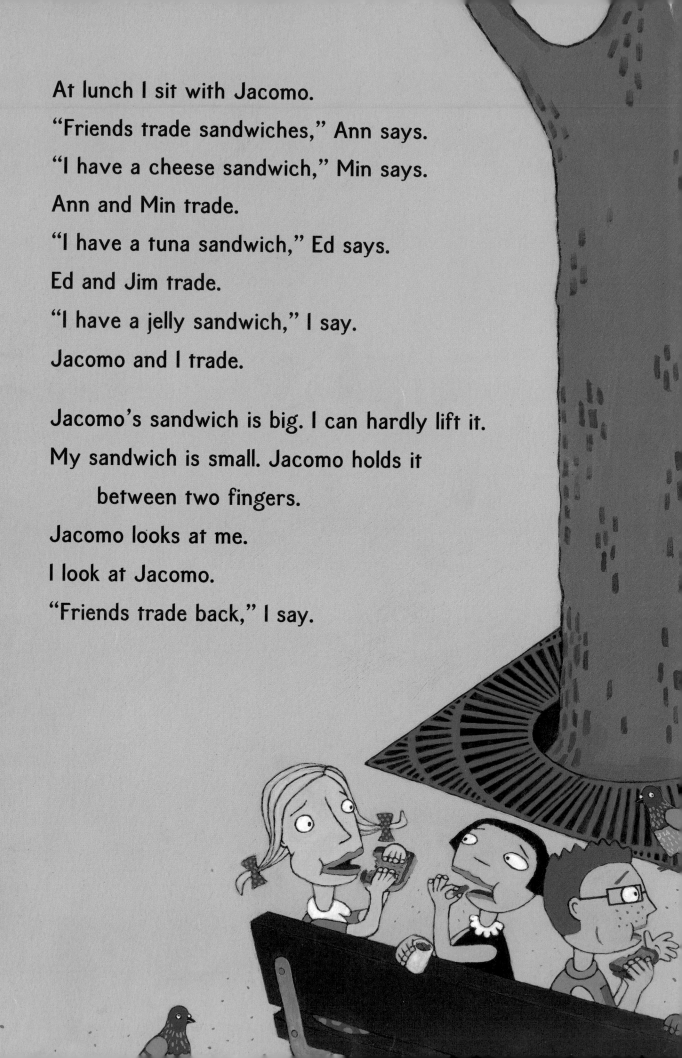

At lunch I sit with Jacomo.

"Friends trade sandwiches," Ann says.

"I have a cheese sandwich," Min says.

Ann and Min trade.

"I have a tuna sandwich," Ed says.

Ed and Jim trade.

"I have a jelly sandwich," I say.

Jacomo and I trade.

Jacomo's sandwich is big. I can hardly lift it.

My sandwich is small. Jacomo holds it
     between two fingers.

Jacomo looks at me.

I look at Jacomo.

"Friends trade back," I say.

After lunch, we go to the library.

Jacomo looks high for a book.

I look low for a book.

Jacomo finds one for me.

I find one for him. I give Jacomo a high five.

He gives me a low five.

The bell rings.

It's time to go home.

I take the bus.

Jacomo waits for me at our bus stop.

We walk home together.
We are best friends, now.

This was a good day.
I have never felt so tall.